Miny Fizz

Flairs and Glairs

Publication House

"Miny Fizz"

ISBN No: " 978-93-90416-97-4"
1st Edition
Language – English and Hindi

Flairs and Glairs
Publication House
Regd. Under MSME Act.

Disclaimer

This is a work of fiction and solely represent the thoughts of the corresponding authors of the articles. Our editors have tried their best to edit the content of all the authors and check the plagiarism.

All the write-ups in this book are unique and are only published in this book.

In case any plagiarism or error is found, only the author is responsible alone, and not the publisher or the Compilers.

Cover Designing
Shubham Shah

Acknowledgement

Dear Almighty, thank you for blessing me with the power and zeal to be able to complete this Anthology. Also, Thank You dear parents, for trusting in me, and letting me work whenever I wanted. My family is the one who supported me for what I am today.
When it comes to this Anthology, I would like to start with Thanking the Co-authors, without your help and support, I would have never been able to complete it.

Thank You all of you, for being there. Much Love to all of You. I am glad to see you all standing by me.

Co Authors

1. Shubham Shah (Founder Flairs and Glairs)
2. Ishani Agarwal (Co Founder Flairs and Glairs)
3. Shivangi Jaiswal (Compiler)
4. Ishani Agarwal
5. Ishika Agarwal
6. Aditya Srivastava
7. Ajay Poddar 'Anmol
8. Heena Shaikh Mulla
9. Arijit Mondal
10. Deepjyoti Chowdhury
11. Bickey Mandal
12. Pragyan Panda
13. Sachin Banoudhiya
14. Subhrajyoti Nanda
15. Abhilash Sharma
16. Yash Ojha
17. Atul Kumar
18. Tanupreet Kaur
19. Dwiza
20. Shreeja Roy
21. Mausam Agrawal
22. Shaily Tyagi
23. Pooja Singh
24. Neha. M
25. Meenakshi Sharma
26. Shajeela Shamreen
27. R.Susanna Celsia
28. Diksha Motwani
29. Shivani Shrikant Sarwade

30.अनिल विश्वकर्मा
31.Jata_V
32.Smriti Kumari
33.Amita Prabhakar
34.Astha Yadav
35.Sakshi Barad
36.Mohua Chakraborty
37.Samikhya Swain
38.Punita Sinha
39.Maitreyee
40.Adarsh Kumar Priyadarshi
41.Avi Srivastava
42.Harshit Kumar
43.Neha Singhania
44.Siya Golani
45.Richie Racheeta
46.Khushbu Rathore
47.Anmol Chugh Dildard
48.Sreelakshmi Viswam
49.Saloni Santosh Gawas
50.Sanoj Kumar
51.Sahina Ghugha
52.Ujjwal Shree
53.Hema Kirthiga J
54.Sanjida Khan
55.Shivansh Sharma
56.Anurag Anan

Shubham Shah

(Founder- Flairs and Glairs)

Shubham Shah, entrepreneur at "Flairs & Glairs" a brand with dynamics in events organizing and cultural educational pan INDIA, He is a 26yr. old guy who recently has entered, the digital platform of imprinting emotions. He has initiated with his own open mic platform to help budding poets and aspiring writers under his brand named as "Teekhe Zasbaaat"

He is a commerce graduate from Bhagalpur City of Bihar.

He says Writing has impersonated him since childhood and he has now been writing for over a decade!

Cooking, on the other hand, is his passion! He also mentions, trying out new things just tickles him!

When asked sir, Why SPICY EMOTIONS?

He smiled and added, "agar jasbaat teekhe na ho toh wo jasbaat kaha" Spices are all that blends! So do his words!

As a chef, he presents to you his dish! Hot and freshly served! Taste it! Feel it! Enjoy it! You can also find his writing in the Solo book "Teekhe Zasbaaat" and 70+ anthologies. With his passion to explore opportunities across Platforms he is working with keen devotion and We wish him all the very best for his future ventures

Share your reviews on his

INSTAGRAM

@spicy_emotions
@shubham4shah

Or via email on

shubham2shah@gmail.com

To stay tuned to his work and opportunities follow his business Handles

INSTAGRAM   FACEBOOK   YOUTUBE

@flairsandglairs
@teekhezasbaaat

WEBSITE:

https://flairsandglairs.in/
https://flairsandglairs.com/

Ishani Agarwal

(Co Founder- Flairs and Glairs)

Ishani Agarwal
Born and brought up in Kolkata, she has done her schooling and college from here itself. She is doing her post-graduation at the moment. Ishani loves talking to people around, and is excited for this new beginning of hers! Been a Compiler for 35+ Anthologies, and in the process for more, also, co-authored in 100+ Anthologies, Ishani is very Happy with how her life is turning out now!
Insta handle: Ishani_agarwal_quotes

Shivangi Jaiswal
(Compiler)

Shivangi Jaiswal is a Content Writer from Kolkata. Project Head & Coordinator at "Flairs & Glairs" brand with dynamics in events organizing and cultural educational pan INDIA.Organiser at "The Glittering Fables" Writing Community. She is a B.Com Honours graduate. Certified in Stocks & Short Selling as well as Certified in Digital Marketing Been a keen student, she has recently been Certified for learning Spanish Language..She loves to bring smiles and happiness to many faces, so she is into social service. Shivangi has also done her Diploma in painting, drawing and all kinds of clay making, craft works. Traveler, Teacher, Meditator, Dancer, Singer, Instrument Player. She loves to play guitar and harmonium. Been a public speaker she has taken part in many events and nailed it. Also been a great

Advisor to many. Sports freak of Swimming and Badminton with a passion so strong. Since, past one year she has started her writing journey. She writes so that many people can connect with their stories and get positive hopes. She thinks " Every story is unique so embrace yourself to the best".She is a writer by day and a reader by night. Been a Complier of 20+ Anthologies, and in process for more, also Co- authored 60+ anthologies.

Shivangi is an old soul with young eyes, a vintage heart,and a beautiful mind."

You can follow her work:

Instagram

@the_knockingvibe

@house_of_compilations

Love Together

Love Together,
Be With you forever.

Your love,
Your life,
Your thoughts
are now mine.
Your look,
your
honestly gives me life.

How often the way you
look at me.
How many times you
smile at me.
Don't know how should
I express my
feelings to you.
The amount of effort
you put for me.
You try again and again
and settle down our fight.
How much you appreciate
all the things.

You took away all the
waves from my life,
And filled with
contentment and joy.
You lifted me and a
whole new me was born.

Forgiveness is hard.

Forgiveness is a gift,
which only a few deserve.
Mistakes happen, but learn to accept it
A wrong word can shatter everything,
where sometimes you can never gain forgiveness again.

It's not easy to forgive someone
when you are hurt or betrayed.
You try to forgive them but your
heart doesn't allow you to do.
Because once the pieces are
broken you cannot mend them again.

The marks on it goes with time.
And it's very hard to let go things..
Never hurt someone you love the most,
that it ruins their happiness
And at last forgiveness is also of no use.

Learn to love,
Learn to forgive
Learn to make a powerful bond
Life is small
Be happy and live happy

Be a Healer.

If one can stop someone from
stepping into the world of thorns.
She shall never go in vain.

If one can erase someone's life scars,
And make it heal.
She will live a new life.

If one can help someone to not sink
and settle,
The sea will never have any storm.

Everything falls in a shower,
don't dissolve in it.
Rather Solve and Survive in It.

.

O life! O life!

Full jar of questions, O life!

With endless paths, looking for the right.
Me myself approaching for "Who Am I?"

For eyes craving for the light, in full of darkness.
Waiting for a sign of hope.

For empty passing years, day by day.
Waiting for a miracle to happen.

Questions revolving round and round.
Struggling for each and every answer.

Life exists, but identify fades.
The powerful game goes on and we fade away.
Yes, Silent and Amazed we fade away.

Aditya Srivastava

Aditya is a future engineer. He had also been part a of 10+ anthologies and writes when he desires to.He wants to make his career in research field and wants to find something great for the good cause of the world.
You can connect to him at: @b.e.z.u.b.a.n__d.i.l

(1)

तेरे जाने के बाद रो गया था,
एक कोने में कैद हो गया था,
तुझे तस्वीरों ने निहार लेता था,
दीवारों पे सर मार लेता था,
टूट कर बिखरा हुआ सब,
मैं सी रहा था,
तेरे हिस्से

(2)

लाखों की भीड़ में जिसको ढूंढ़ लू
वो सुरत तेरी है..
पूरी दुनिया को एक ओर रख जिस से मौहबत कर लू
वो आंखे तेरी है....
यूं जिदंगी... जीने के दिन तो नहीं मेर

Ajay Poddar 'Anmol

He is Ajay Poddar 'Anmol' from kolkata, mainly his most of works started from Uttrakhand he used to live in Madhyapradesh he is the only person in his family who loves literature because he thinks only literature and positive literacy can change the world and society after 7 years of struggle he entered in literature fully by professional development from dream analysis,

He want to proof that universal fact literature is directly proportional to scienc

e and science is directly proportional to god and god is directly proportional to literature ,

Ana Usi Kinare

Kabhi manjil se dur kabhi manjil ke karib mila mujhe,
Tumse milkar mera hi tasveer mila mujhe,
Dard ka hal to atit ban gaya,
Tumse milkar marham dene wala hakim mila mujhe,
Khamoshi pyari thi tum usse pyari ho,
Sabse chup chap hokar mujhse batein karne wali ho,
Tumhe pakar khoya hua takdir mila mujhko,
Jo haar ko hara de wo lakir mila mujhko,
Ghulkar tum mei hi kahi mujhe mein mila hu,
Kanto sa tha tumhare ane se ful sa khila mein,
Dosti thi lakho se,
mohabbat mili tumhari ankho se,
Barish ki pehli bund thi teri dosti,
Ab mohabbat indra dhanush sa hai,
Pehle 'Anmol' mafia sa tha,
Tumse milkar ab bhadr manush sa hai,
Ana usi kinare par mathe ko sahlane,
Dur kar sitam ki duniya se khudko,
Dubkar is ghadi se mujhme samane,

Heena Shaikh Mulla

Heena Shaikh Mulla is from Pune,currently residing in Karnataka.
She's from an ICSE background,graduated from Pune University(MSC Computer Science). She's the author of 'Technical Desserts' and also hold a Vajra record for the same.
Besides being a college topper,She likes drawing henna,teaching and fantasizes about Polar Bears.
She's a charming personality who expresses her thoughts in the form of Poetry and Shayri and currently she's compiling books as well.

An Ode to Freedom

Oh dear freedom,
Thank you for giving me the liberty,
Right after I reached my puberty.

Oh dear freedom,
Thank you for this kingdom,
Where I can freely share my wisdom.

Oh dear freedom,
Thank you for giving me my rights,
And making me capable to fight.

Oh dear freedom,

Thank you for providing me with the basic necessities of mankind,
Now I feel so connected and twined.

Oh dear freedom,
I owe to you to utilize you efficiently,
And come out of it proficiently.

Arijit Mondal

Arijit Mondal ,a boy with big dreams. He is very much hardworking and energetic guy and a reliable friend to hand around. He is a bookaholic in nature and loves to pen down his feelings. He believes hardwork is the major key to success .

You, My Unfulfilled Desire

Our life is very strange. There is big difference between the thoughts of that time and the thoughts of today.

We have done a lot of things since childhood that are very disappointing .There have been many such incidents in my life .What once gave me so much joy is now a source of shame to me .These are the biggest mistakes of my life .The mistakes didn't seem wrong to me then .In fact, reality was behind my eyes ,There was a lot of emotions .Remember ,these two things are parallel, can never be united .The role of these two in our lives is undeniable .We have to create balance between the two .

If I had understood then, life might have been different .Maybe you stay in my life .These were the best days of my life when I talked to you .Maybe love was one-sided, but it was an endless desire for me to talk to you ,which may not be possible right now .Never said it to anyone because love doesn't have to be public ,But I don't know why I miss you so much today, so I have recorded you on my notebook .

Deepjyoti Chowdhury

Deepjyoti Chowdhury embraces reading and writing as her escape from the real world as well as a window to it. She is a strong believer of Christ and Karma. Written in 100+ anthologies, she is the author of "Heartfelt musings" and "The staircase to freedom". Her main aim is to heal people and make them smile through her art of writing. You can follow her on Instagram at dj_writes_to_heal .

Crystal Clear

The truth to me is now crystal clear,
It makes us stronger, every pain we bear.
The tormentation makes our vision unclear,
After the storm the result clearly appear.

To be a rebel first you need to shed tear,
Then kill negativity and all sort of fear.
The rules of universe you need to adhere,
Faithfully you need to be wise and sincere.

You would be protected with guidance and shelter,
When helpless you would be sent a helper.
You don't fall that is what matters,
To make you tough, sometimes the world shatters.

One day, it all makes sense;
It was all a planned journey from heaven.
Forget the pain and see through a colourful lens,
Colourful and bright would look the entire nation.

Bickey Mandal

He is Bickey Mandal from Jharkhand. Now he is in the last semester of his graduation from B.B.M.K.U Dhanbad with English Honours. With his poetries he trying to connect himself with others. He is passionate about his works because he love what he do. He have a stedy source of motivations that drives him to do his best. He wants to became a writer from last 5 year so, he collect his Thoughts, Poetry and Lyrics from then to make a good book in his both books he presenting many beautiful shayari, Love quotes , Motivational quotes & sad stories. You can contact him through instagram at @bickey_ki_ankahi_baatein
E-mail- bickeymandal91@gmail.com

(1)

The flower of happiness,
are not to bound a season.
It blooms out of season.
And spread the fragrance of love.

Happiness is not just a word.
It is priceless for the sad ones.
Who never happy because of,
Their self thinking & ego .

For me happiness is my World,
Where my family exist.
They try to make everything possible
For me that gives me happy.

Beauty of happiness,
Is the essence of life.
That fragrance our life,
With joy and peaceful.

With a cute smile face,
We can win everyone's heart.
This is the nature of smile.
This is the power of smile.

Pragyan Panda

Pragyan is persuing her B.Tech in "Chemical Engineering" from IGIT, Sarang. She's a short girl from Rourkela, Odisha. With fascination of nature, she's a spiritual person who motivates people. She does weird stuff like interacting with non living ones and pens down her mind. For more of her works, do follow her IG @quote_love_97.

Feelings: Thou Complex

Suppose a melody;
Or a tired and accused weirdly:
A horrific day at the end.
Well it's because you aren't dead.

Suppose a blissful shower;
The victory of power!!
Sensible pain with memories_
No rest but repeating stories.

Depends on clothing and food;
The moulded delicate mood.
A happy or a sad soul moves on;
A kick and always a lesson.

To express is human;
Be overexposed is insane_
How complex and varying unsteady:
Well its common to all; kind of moody.

Sachin Banoudhiya

He is a student of Bsc
A Struggling Writer now Started Getting so many platforms
He Loves to do Audio Poetries & video Editing.
He's a Publish Co - author in so many Anthologies

अभी तन्हा हूं मैं

मंज़िल से जरा कह दो, अभी पहुंचा नही हूं मैं
कदमो को बांध न पाएंगी, मुसीबत कि जंजीरें,
रास्तों से जरा कह दो, अभी भटका नही हूं मैं
सब्र का बांध टूटेगा, तो फ़ना कर के रख दूंगा,
दुश्मन से जरा कह दो, अभी गरजा नही हूं मैं
दिल में छुपा के रखी है, लड़कपन कि चाहतें,
मोहब्बत से जरा कह दो, अभी बदला नही हूं मैं
साथ चलता है, दुआओ का काफिला
किस्मत से जरा कह दो, अभी तनहा नही हूं मैं....

Main Jeet Kar Dikhaunga

Padhna Likhna To Zindagi Bhar Chalega
Zindagi Me Aish Krna Bhi Zaruri Hai
Future Ko "BAHOT HARD"
Banana hai
Itne Se mEra kuch Nahi hoga
Thodi or problems aayengi
Aane Do
Thodha Or Time Lagega
Lagne Do
Thodha Or effort Lagenge Lagaunga
Par is baar To Main Jeet Kar Dikhaunga

Subhrajyoti Nanda

Subhrajyoti Nanda is a 17 years old student from Odisha,a published co author in many anthologies,a district level debator, a state level essay writing winner and also loves to host, dance and sing.She feels, writing exhibits his beats and she was inspired by her father,who is himself a poet and the ink inspires her in her own ways.She has received many awards in these fields and aims to shape the society with her positive perspective and unconditional kindness.

Miny Fizz

The Voice Against Dowry!

Her bright beautiful eyes upon her rosy bridely cheeks
Rolled tears of abuse and punishment like bitter wine,
Ending her own existence,shreding her marriage's mortality
Staining her in minutes, deep within!

Is dowry a necessity;
with the pious relationship of love and times?
Damn your narrow minded senses,
Burn thou selfish,harsh money capturing minds.

Is marriage either a business or a pardon?
Is that a way to kill someone each day, for gulping much
lumpsome bribe?
Begging each such questions
What else stays alive?

Is there a reason
To support this crime?
To destroy all relationships,serenity and faith
And fear no demise?

Is her life, her parents'love is just worth the 'so called dowry',
Some jewelleries,some properties,
some money,
Is it all what she needs to keep as a claim for her life;
Is it what that would make her die hopelessly,sitting on knee?

So, dear people,I beg near you!

Keep your breathes with love,as your soul is so dead,
Don't weigh love with money,don't stay silent, as Almighty
hath said. From devils,Be men and pamper the daughters of
heaven,

Slaughter the souls,salivating for bribes, as your greatest
treasure has already been taken!

One ray of awareness, another of conscience,
Embrace the girl wealth,glowy divine,yes our silvery lines!
On this Earth, stop bidding the priceless lives of girls with
mere money,
Raise your voice,know the righteousness and make happy
lives shine!

Abhilash Sharma

Abhilash Sharma a 23 year old passionate writer. He belongs to Sonipat , Haryana . He had completed his B.com (voc) recently. He is a enthusiastic person and a sports lover as well .Worked as a co author in about 50+ anthologies inspired by Ishika Arora and Ishani Aggarwal in the field of writing .You can check out his writings on instagram at @_ankahe_alfaaz__ .

वापसी :- मेरा जूनून

मेरे हाल पर हँसने वाले ,
मुझे यूँ धकेलने वाले ,
इतना कमजोर समझने वाले ,
हारा हुआ सोचने वाले ,

ये शेर अभी वापिस आएगा ,
सबको अपना रूप दिखाएगा ,
दिलो में सबके वो बस जाएगा ,
गौरव सबका वो जरूर लाएगा ।।

Yash Ojha

He is "Yash Ojha" son of 'Dr. Ram Sahay Ojha' and 'Mrs. Usha Ojha' , born and raised in Ayodhaya, UP. He completed his schooling from Udaya Public School and now is pursuing Graduation in Arts(hons.) with English currently. He has a Degree in Hacking field as well. Writing was not a profession but somehow became passion for him. Now he has completed his own 30+ Poetries as well. The flow of his words seemed effortless, and before he knew about it. It had grown beyond this many poetries which was on his hands. He received so much encouragement and positive feedbacks from his parents and others and then he found that he shouldn't stop writing.

"Light Me Up Like"
(Dedicated to Mom)

With your smile I forgot everything about stress and tension of working....

You make me believe that everything is possible in front of your focused mind....

You also make me believe that no one can take you to the road of success; it's just only you who can do it for yourself...

The life outside home from 8 to 2 everyday; but on Sunday I feel that how much I am lucky to have you in my life....

It was such a shame feeling for me that I think that I can't do anything in my life....

> "But you came to light up my life...
> You brought in me faith; hope; love and light"!!!....

Atul Kumar.

He is Atul Kumar. He has experience of compiling one anthology titled Dream We All Have.

(1)

Love is lifeline
Love is lifeline to happiness .
Love is to live the life with some craziness .
Love keep us cool and calm .
Love is a way to kickout the tension .

Love means to treats everyone equally .
Love motivates to achieve something bigger in life .
Love makes your thinking smart .
Loves increase your creativity and art.

Tanupreet Kaur

Tanupreet Kaur is born and brought up in New Delhi, India and a graduate in bachelor of arts along with the certification in Creative Writing, German Language and Desktop Publishing. She has been writing since 2016 to achieve the expression of her life and finding solace. She started this journey with writing quotes firstly then poetry and finally short stories and to know her more you can check her instagram handle : @_heavenofdiversions_

Why ? Why ! Why.

Why to blend ?
When you are here to stand out.

Why to repress ?
When you can be sprout.

Why to deject ?
When you can have no doubt.

Why to isolate ?
When you can scout.

Why to copy ?
When you can be you throughout.

Dwiza

This Is Dwiza Daughter Of Mr. Pardeep Kalra And Mrs. Devinder Writing is never made to do, It just happens. I never had any inspiration of writing. My inner feelings made me this capable. I wish to write further and get a name for myself by this passion of mine.
 You can visit her online on Instagram @Silhouette__Emotions

आखिर कौन हूँ मैं ?

कोन हूँ में क्या पहचान है मेरी,
क्या खुद को जानती हूँ में
या यूं लिखती फिरती
कतरा-कतरा,जरा जरा,
इस जालिम जिन्दगी का,
जो खुद को कागज पे उतारती हूँ मैं,
क्या वक़्त हैं मेरे पास खुद से मिलने का,
क्या जीना बखुबी जानती हूँ मैं,
एक सवाल उस वक़्त उठ जागा करता है,
जब थक के सुकून से बैठी होती हूं मैं,
एक हड़कंप सा सिने में मच जाया करता है,
इसी सवाल पर की,
आखिर कौन हूँ मैं
आखिर कौन हूँ मैं

मैं थोड़ी अजीब सी लड़की हूं

मैं थोड़ी अजीब सी लड़की हूं
मैं अंधेरों से रोशनी की बातें करती हूं
धूप से छांव की बातें करती
सुबह से रात की बातें करती हूँ
और रात से सुबह की बातें करती हूं
पानी से आग की बातें करती हूं
और आग से पानी की बातें करती हूं
में कहानी से किरदारों की बातें करती हूं
किरदार से कहानी की बातें करती हूँ
में थोड़ी अजीब सी लड़की हूं
में दिल से रूह की बातें करती हूं
और रूह से दिल की बातें करती हूं
तुम जानते हो मैं तुमसे मेरी बातें करती हूं
और खुद से तेरी बातें करती हूं
और रात को आते है जो चाँद सितारे
उनसे हमारी बाते करती हूँ..
हां! मैं थोड़ी अजीब सी लड़की हूं

Shreeja Roy

Shreeja Roy is an English Literature student at Rabindra Bharati University, Kolkata. She loves writing and has published her works in Akara monthly magazines, she has co-authored 10+ anthologies so far. Instagram Id- @shreejaroy1999

A Dreamer Is Never Lost

He yelled hard, " You are responsible for all today!" ,
pointing the most beautiful woman I know,
 whose tears feed me immense pain, she's my Mom.
"One must cut his coat according to the cloth,
and your son is lost in impossible dreams.
He's a vagabond! A wanderer!
 Who couldn't qualify the Engineering Entrance.
No IIT, no future. Haven't I said?"
This is what I always heard- No IIT, no future.
"But he loves music and I know he will succeed", she claimed.
He slapped her, and that was something I couldn't stand.
I held her hand, and she trusted me,
With my Mom and my guitar, I left home that day.
Her fingers ached, I know, when she tailored to earn,
to buy me the guitar that I wanted.
I couldn't let her efforts ever go in vain.
Four years hence, waits the audience,
to have my presence on stage.
A crowd of thousands cheering around,
there in front, sits my Mom, happy and proud.
She believed, though I wandered but I won't be lost.
The event ends, towards my car I head,
" Sir, autograph please!", a voice interrupted,
a very known voice, apologetic eyes, I couldn't resist myself,
I hugged him, " I missed you, Dad. I am not lost,
I was never lost, I was just a dreamer.
And a dreamer is never lost"

Doll

I remember my friend calling me for company,
to be a hand in her doll's marriage ceremony.
We were seven and we hardly knew what marriage really meant,
Her doll was about to marry the one her uncle had sent.
"Give me her jewellery, the groom is waiting!"
She said, but something inside kept me hunting.
"Why do I feel Sara your doll is upset?
Have you asked her will before making the marriage all set?"
" What to ask? It's my decision.
I am her guardian and she is my possession.
'Girls cannot decide', my parents say,
They should always adapt to whatever comes their way"
"But the doll's eyes, you see, are about to shed tears,
She is unwilling to marry, please try to hear!"
" It's nothing my friend, what's the use of delay?
She can neither speak nor hear, it's a doll by the way."
I threw flowers on the doll's marriage that day,
And the same I am about to do again today.
A decade passed, and it's Sara's turn,
to tie the knot and get back the return.
I went to the room where the bride was dressed.
She looked like a beautiful doll heavily jewelled.
But her eyes seemed similar to those of the doll,
whose marriage ceremony was attended by us all.
She called me aside, and said shedding a drop of tear,
"I wish, that day, what the doll said, I could hear."

Mausam Agrawal

She is 22 year old girl from Nepal and has completed her graduation from Kolkata.She loves writing its her passion .She has written poems,shayaris and stories.

Use Of Brains

The era of techonology
Has reduced the use of brains
People are just grown into the puppet of
Human invent
Now they don't remember the simple dates
all of them are saved
The more the techonology grew
The more people became its slave
All the work is so easy and faster
That machines leads to human disaster
Employees are fired and machines are hired
Use of brain is not acknowledged
But this techonology is a outcome of human brain
If used properly ,we can overcome all the odds
So give importance to creativity and people
Who use brain for good of people.

Chai Pehla Pyaar

Woh kulaad wali chai ho kisi tapri pe pee hui
Yaa bin mausam barsaat mai
Pakore ke sath chuski wali
Woh chai woh rishte ki shuruwat ki
Yaa thori si bachi pocket money ke tang halat ki
Jab bhi uss chai ka
Sawad aata hai labo pe
Ek alag si khusi milti hai
Haaye yeh chai kya khoob lagti hai

Sar dard mitana ho
Ya phir tension ko bhagna ho
Dur se iski khusboo
Hone ka ahsas dilati hai
Yeh yunhi nahi pehla pyaar kehlati hai

Shaily Tyagi

She is Shaily Tyagi, a born writer.
She is always ready to face challenges and gives her best in every field.
She is a compiler, loves to compile different feelings of different hearts.
Here she is with her beautiful poem, hope all will love to read.

Fizz of life

For me mini fizz is just like a dream that comes suddenly and Awake me from the darkness of the life, the darkness in which we lost some time and we never could find a right path.

 or I must say it is like a sparkling water that gives an intense peace to my mind and to my soul and make me calm whenever I see such water waves ,it is just like a peace in my mind.
 whenever you go to such a place, you will feel Calmness in your mind and heart and you will get an enthusiasm to do, whatever you want to do you, with the high spirit .

it is like a river that is forming and gives different meaning to life that all good things or bad things will decay one day and all new things will take place.

Pooja Singh

Pooja Singh stays in Mumbai the place she loves to be.She's pursuing dentistry as a profession.
But besides that she likes to express her emotions and thoughts through poems.
She writes on many genres specially on women empowerment.
She prefers writing her own creation.
And hope to reach hearts of the readers.
She believes in philosophy that "Happiness is an inside job".

Life in Urban Jungle

Life in urban jungle
There's sound everywhere,
no silence no peace.
Nobody's moving their feets,
just sitting and staring the screen.
The food's stale, no health no gain.
The air is polluted, no freshness just bare.
The life is sold in money here,
the poor has lost believe.
Man is engaged in sadness and cruelty.
why man no mission for peace?
Why there's no compassion?
Why just Success is in the air?
why there's no love and romance.
just love is a hard catch to find.
Well man there's always a better
way just follow the lead of the divine.

Neha. M

Meet this Biomedical Engineer from Mumbai who says that though her profession claims practicality but words have always beckon her emotionally. She belives it's only the art who has no confinement on expression.

Depression

Dear depressed,

I like everyone cannot assure you to be always there for you considering the uncertainty of my own life and situation but I know one thing...

That the city that's build up with so many stories

Can always battle one more of your story.

In a million trillion of ears everywhere

there can always be one that takes a stride of being your listener.

Yes, we all know 'vulnerabilities' are so judgmental but remember never worthier than anyone's life.

So let's have some free sunlight with a loud shameful conversation than a room of darkness with a silent screams.

(2)

Aaj ek naye shaher ka darwaza khatkhataya,

Kehte hai yaha kuch khaas log rehte hai.

Mehfilo mein sunni thi kahaniya inki,

Yaha gehre sanaate ke alawa kuch bhi nahi hai.

Awaazein jaisi kho he gayi ho humesha ke liye.

Sunna h ek safar wo bhi toh hai

jaha pair nahi dil thakta hai;

Shayad wo sabhi log yahi baste hai.

Aaj isliye ek naye shaher ka darwaza khatkhataya,

Kya pata shayad mann lag jaye idhar he…

Meenakshi Sharma

Meeakshi Sharma, a keen writer, thinks that God sends us on earth with full of strength. And we are eble to find whatever we want with our superb will power.

(1)

तुमको मिल कर ही तो यह जाना है,
कितना सुंदर यह जमाना है,
हम इस दुनिया में आखिर क्यों आए हैं
तुमसे ही तो रिश्ता कोई पुराना है

चांद गवाह है इन बातों का, जो मेरे
तुम्हारे हैं, उन् एहसासों का,
तुमको ही तो हमने बस अपना जाना है,
बस इतनी हकीकत बाकी फसाना है

अजी इस जहां में और रखा क्या है
तुमसे मिलने की आरजू लेकर
हमने छोड़ दिया जमाना है
चलें आएं है तुम्हारे लिए
हर वादा हमें निभाना है

रिश्ते निभाना चांद से हमने सीखा है
 जो मिलने अपने प्रियतम से रोज आता है
 ना कोई गिला न कोई शिकवा है छिपा
जो निभाता है वह प्यार का वादा है
 वही रिश्ता निभाना हमने भी चाहा है
बस अब जो कहा करके भी दिखाना है
तुमको मिलकर ही तो ये जाना है
 कितना सुंदर ये जमाना है।।

Shajeela Shamreen

Shajeela shamreen is a co author of many anthologies.she is currently pursuing a undergraduate degree in literature.she is on the process of becoming a well defined writer and soon she will achieve it. A strong dreamer basically,who wants to make those dreams true soon.

Literature- The Art Of Life

Literature is a mirror of life
Which shows the world entirely
It has many aspects
Through which one can see,
Life,Art,Career etc.,
And travel through it
Literature shows you the ways,
You can go through it,
Return from it,
Anything can be done
One who chooses literature
They choose the reality of life
Because literature depicts life
They learn love,hostility,treachery
Sadness, joyfulness
Everything in one
It opens many people's minds
To see the world's reality
One learns to not to judge anyone
By first impression
One cannot force their own perspectives
On another, because
Literature gives free choice
To one and all
One can expose their talents,
One learns to live their life;
Literature is different from other genres
It has a great depth
Which none can explore
Thoroughly.

R.Susanna Celsia

A passionate writer and published poet and blogger who aspires to touch lives through her writings,she writes from her life experiences ,that is not only inspiring but also makes it a savoury to the soul

Happy Pill

Sometimes we really need to stop and take a happy pill!!!
Anger ,frustration, failure and negativity encircles and
suffocates taking the life out of us and replacing it with
posion.
And happiness is out of the list ,
In moments like this stop !! And find a reason to be happy
,take a happy pill
Sometimes we are so much filled with peoples words
,reputation, expectations and situations,
A reason to be happy i find not ,thats when you need to stop
!! And find a reason to be happy ,take a happy pill
Sometimes all we can hear ,touch and feel is our failures and
depression ,depriving us
You can still find a reason to be happy ,take a happy pill

Diksha Motwani

Diksha is a moody girl. She use to write. She use to pen her thoughts when she feels happiest, saddest, depressed. Her pen is her best friend. She believes that writing is a best way to express the thoughts and views. She believes that karma is a bitch. So she keeps herself on peace and calm and let karma do his work. She is a commerce student.(11th standard). She lives in Ulhasnagar, Mumbai. Her dad and her best friend are her motivators. She appreciates the patience level of her dad. She believes that instead of doing a war, do express by penning the thoughts. She is having a goal to be a CA. Besides writing, she practice arts, calligraphy and singing.

Merrily Messed Yet Blessed

Girl quite introvert,
Usually pens extrovert.
Life fully messed,
Yet she is self-obsessed.
Crying for her past dont know why,
But surely she never said a lie.
Loves to sing freely,
Lives her life limitlessly.
Bit innocent and cute,
But sometimes rude.
Her patience is on another level,
So dont let her lose it ever.
She is beloved of lord Ganesha,
Loved by all of her true friends.
She is me!
Yes that girl is me!

Shivani Shrikant Sarwade

Shivani, a future pharmacist living in the city of God Vitthala-Pandharpur.She is an ambitious girl who follows her heart and loves to write what her heart says!! Student of science but also admirer of arts too. She can sense God in her parents along with that she believes in love, kindness and humanity too.

"बेशुमार"

चाहत बेशुमार है हमसे फिर भी,
हमारे दहलीज पें खड़े हो।

हमारा दिल कोई और ले गया,
शायद यही सोचकर
अपनी जिद पर अड़े हो।

"क्या मिला??"

दौलत का चांद ,,
शौहरत की चांदनी ...

इन्हे ही पाने के लिए
तुम गये थे हमे छोड़कर ...

हम तो बस्स अब मुस्कुराते है
तुम्हारे ये हालात देख-देखकर ...

क्या मिला ??
ना वो "चांद" ना ये
खूबसूरत सी "चांदनी"...
कुछ भी तो नही।

"जख़्म"

दिल संभल रहा था
दिल के छा़लों पर "मल्हम"
लगने ही वाला था,
घाँव भरने ही लगे थे,,,
और
वह वापस आ गया...

मसीहा बनकर नही,
उन जख़्मों को फिर से
ताजा करने के लिए ही,
वह वापस आया था...

दिल संभल रहा था

अनिल विश्वकर्मा

लेखक को श्री अनिल कुमार विश्वकर्मा के नाम से जाना जाता है, वे देश की राजधानी दिल्ली से सम्बन्ध रखते हैं। उनकी स्नातक की शिक्षा दिल्ली विश्वविद्यालय से हुई है तथा वर्तमान में वे एक प्रतिष्ठित संगठन में कार्यरत हैं। वे एक गम्भीर व ज़िम्मेदार युवक होने के साथ-साथ कर्तव्यनिष्ठ और पारिवारिक व्यक्ति भी हैं। अपने जीवन के दैनिक कार्यों में व्यस्त रहते हुए भी वे अपनी लेखन रुचि को जीवित रखते हैं। अपने स्नातकोत्तर के दौरान ही उनमें लेखन की रुचि उत्पन्न हो गई थी, किंतु इस कला को भौतिक स्वरूप देने में उन्हें कुछ समय लगा। उनके लेखन की प्रेरणा व स्रोत उनकी प्रिय जीवनसंगिनी है। वे थोड़े अल्पभाषी है किंतु कलम के माध्यम से वे अपनी बात कहना जानते हैं। वे अपनी रचनाओं और लेखनी के माध्यम से आप लोगों से जुड़ना चाहते हैं तथा साथ ही साथ यह भी कामना करते हैं कि आप लोगों का प्रोत्साहन व स्नेह भी उन्हें भरपूर मिले क्योंकि वे इस क्षेत्र में अभी नवीन हैं परंतु इस यात्रा में और आगे तक जाने की इच्छा रखते हैं।

लॉकडाउन।

कभी नहीं देखा था ऐसा बुरा मंज़र,
जैसा लॉकडाउन ने हम सबको है दिखलाया,
नोटबंदी तो हुई थी कुछ समय पहले,
इस बार कोरोना ने पूरा देश ही बंद करवाया,
किया हम सब को घर में जो कैद,
बाहर निकलना, और घूमना तक बंद करवाया,
बाल बढ़वाकर बना दिया हमें साधु,
सिनेमा, पार्टी और मौज-मस्ती सब बंद करवाया,
दूध-सब्ज़ी, दवा-दारू तो बिक रहे हैं,
चाट-पकोड़े और होटल का खाना ही बंद करवाया,
रोज़ ऑफिस जाने से दिया छुटकारा,
घर से ही हमसे ऑनलाइन सारा काम करवाया,
पैसे-वालों को तो ले आया बाईज्जत,
कुछ दुखियारों को मुलुक तक पैदल ही चलवाया,
कुछ को तो दिया गया भर पेट भोजन,
कुछ मजबूर गरीब मज़दूरों को भूखों ही मरवाया,
भरत-मिलाप देख रहे थे कुछ घर बैठे,
उधर इसने अपनों को ही अपनों से दूर करवाया,
चले गए थे हम कहीं दूर खुद से ही,
इस लॉकडाउन ने हमको फिर हमीं से मिलवाया।

Jata_V

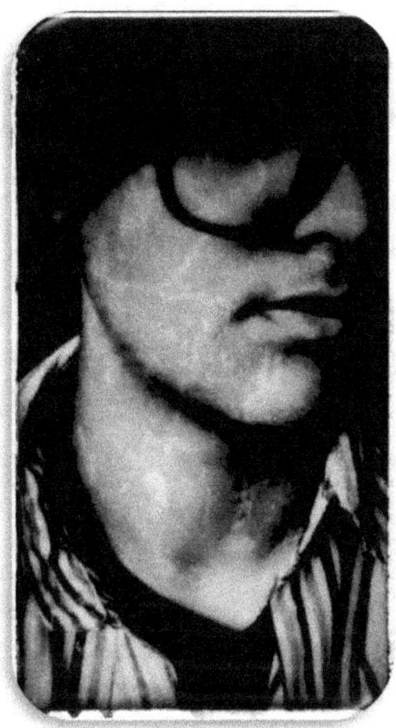

Jata_V, an instrument of Nature, existing in the Indian subcontinent. Time's person of the year 2006, Jata doesn't have a heart of its own. Alien to selfish Love and fellow human expressions. Currently Moonwalking at the tributary where fantasy stream merges with roller coaster life.

Jibri: A Dark Story Of Daulatdia's Dark Girl

No decent guy would go there. Daulatdia, Bangladesh, the town full of colorful prostitutes and hungry men, mostly drivers of the local lorry sheds. "You've got no other place on Earth to make a documentary?", Vishwa yelled at me. I wanted to document the daily routine of the children of Daulatdia 's prostitutes. "No Jata! Forget about it, I'm not coming with you, I'm not like you, I have a girlfriend, yaar! Just think about what Janu would say if she knows about this", Vishwa gave me a hard time packing up for a one-week-long trip. Papers got done, reached there, and incredibly all the locals were so used to Camera-people like us. We reached the target spot finally and right away started shooting the streets, garbage piles, lorry stands, and everything to picturize the actual Daulatdia.

As we didn't want to waste our time in unwanted spots, we went straight to the school in Daulatdia. Save the Children, a global NGO has arranged the school and teachers especially to educate Daulatdia 's children, children who know a way more than what they should know, children who know that their mother is a prostitute, and children who have seen their sisters go with another guy...As we expected the school was mostly filled with boys and only 1 or 2 girls. I wanted to talk with the girls, they've asked two girls named Sonal and Jibri to come to the room where we interviewed the staff. Sonal was bright and got glistening eyes and so we interviewed her and it was almost 4pm. So we decided to pack up our shoot, thanked the staffs, and left the school. As we approached the gate, a kid shouted, "Hey! You Aliens!", in the local language. That was Jibri.

"Hey li'l girl, you want chocolate?", I gave her a chocolate bar. She asked, "Why did you speak only with Sonal, why not me?", she slammed. I and Vishwa got no answer and we saw each other's faces. "I came to school because no boy chose me to have sex with, just because I'm so dark. They all wanted my sister who is lighter than me, they chose her...Just Like You Chose Sonal Now..

Smriti Kumari

Smriti kumari is student by profession,writer by passion.she lives
in New Delhi,india.She is 2nd year student, pursuing bsc(h) maths
from Rajdhani college,Delhi University. She is an optimistic,
passionate, inquisitive and hardworking.she is working as co-
author in many anthologies.The pen is a strong weapon for her to
portray her feelings.she loves to write in her spare time.Friends
and parents are the biggest support of her.let's enjoy her writing

Pehli Mulakat

तेरी तलब को दफना दूं, शायद!
आगोश के एहसास को भूला दूं ,शायद!
ग़म- ए- दिल को भी मना लू, शायद!
 पर कैसे?
बेताबी में चूपी उस बंदगी को भूल जाऊ?
कैसे?
महज़ मुसाफ़िर के हमराज बनने की सफर
को मिटा दूं?
कैसे?
उन प्यारे लम्हों को यादों के भवंडर में खोने दूं?
कैसे?
उस पहली मुलाकात को इस कदर दफन होने दूं?
शायद!
तेरी कशिश ,तेरी हसरत अभी भी खत्म नहीं हुई!
तेरी पहली मुलाक़ात की फितूर अभी दफन नहीं हुई!

Amita Prabhakar

Amita Prabhakar, is a young and dynamic lady in her early 30's. She belongs to the 'Jhoomka' city of Bareilly. She has just completed her B.Ed exams from MJPRU. A bubbly girl who loves to write, who writes to express, her written expressions always impress. She is determined to bring the best out of her. She loves traveling like hell, she has the quantum of everlasting quest when it comes to explore places. She loves to spend the life not for mearly 'chalta hai' attitude rather she takes her life as an opportunity to know the world and make the world see through her tiny window which she has created.She is a lovely mother of two childrens. They are still in their first stages of life spending most of the time exploring between their school bag and lunch box. She is very fond of teaching kids, her array in teaching is magnanimous. She believes that the life is a journey till pyre and we are mare passingers.

Power of Woman

Power of Woman

Don't underestimate the power of woman...
Everyday woman play with knife in the kitchen. So that she knows, How to use weapons?
Everyday woman do physical exercises by doing household work like mopping, wiping , dusting and washing clothes etc. So that women are physically fit, they know How to fight in the battle.
Don't underestimate the power of woman...
Woman have tolerance power also because they know How to handle excessive pain when giving birth to baby?
Woman knows How to tackle the problems of their life.
From above statements it is clear that woman have power to fight against injustice. So don't think women are weak. They are strongest power of the world.
That's why
Don't underestimate the power of woman...

Astha Yadav

Astha Yadav is from Uttar Pradesh. She's an amateur writer who loves to spill her emotions on the pages of her diary. Astha has participated in more than fifty books as a co-author including record holder books. She has compiled eight books till date. She's a vajra world records holder herself. Her only dream is to make her parents proud and happy.
Insta id- red_rose431

जब-जब कोई लड़की

जब-जब कोई लड़की,
किसी के प्रेम में पड़ जाती है,
आंखों से आंखें मिलते ही,
धड़कनें तेज़ हो जाती हैं।
आवाज में जो उसकी मिश्री है,
वह और भी मीठी हो जाती है।।

जब-जब कोई लड़की,
किसी के प्रेम में पड़ जाती है,
ना दिन में सुकून मिलता है,
ना रात को नींद आती है।
एक और मुलाकात की खातिर,
वह बेचैन हो जाती है ।।

जब-जब कोई लड़की,
किसी के प्रेम में पड़ जाती है,
उसकी खुशी की ख़ातिर,
वह हर डर से लड़ जाती है ।
हाथों में हाथ लेकर जब वह आंखों में देखा करते हैं,
एक पल को मानो, उसकी सांसे ही थम जाती हैं।।

जब-जब कोई लड़की,
किसी के प्रेम में पड़ जाती है,
उस पर विश्वास कर,
वह दिन को भी रात बताती है।
उसकी ज़िन्दगी के सुख, दुख,
हर उतार चढ़ाव को वह अपनाती है।।

Sakshi Barad

She is postgraduate student who is writer,author,compiler and orator also.She has more than 10 years experience of writing.She is shayara who performed in many events and like to entertain people with her poetries and shayaris.She is couthor of many books.She is state level orator/public speaker.She has won many trophies in state level elocution and debate competitions.She belevies in hardwork and hold many dreams in eyes and beleives it will come true one day definately.

कौन है वो..?

मेरी कलम अक्सर पुछा करती है..
किसके लिए लिखती हो इतना
उसे भुला नही सकती तो,
हमेशा यूही मेरा सहारा लेती हो..

कौन है वो...?

है शायद कोई अनदेखा अनसुनासा,
है शायद कोई गीत कोई गझलसा,
है शायद कोई थोडा भोला थोडा मासूमसा,
वो मेरा कुछ नहीं पर अपनसा..

कौन है वो...?

वो शायरी है मेरी पर शायर नहीं..
जादू है उसकी हंसी और बातो मे पर वो जादुगार नहीं...!

है कोई वो...

शायद दोस्त या अजनबी अनजानासा,
या फिर या फिर शायद कोई नहीं..!!

खैरियत

आज के बाद आपकी पुछने की हिम्मत नहीं होगी हमारी
क्यूकी...
अच्छे हो कह दोगे तो बिखर जाऐंगे हम...
और बुरे हो कह दोगे तो सहम जाऐंगे हम...!!

गुरूर

आजतक खुदको अच्छेसे पहचान ना सके हम...
और वो कहते है बहोत गुरूर है हमे खुदपर...!!

तेरी आवाज

तेरी आवाज मे कोई तो जादू था...
युही नहीं वो मेरी कानोमें गुंजती है....!!

Shijin Ravi C

He is Mr. Shijin Ravi C from Kerala.He is pursuing BSc
IIons Agriculture graduate.He is a young poet and co-author
of many anthologies today. Some of his anthologies are 'The
golden words','The uncertain periods','My success
ladder','Safar','Her voice','Positive vibes' etc .His mail ID is
shijinravi23@gmail.com . His Instagram ID is stolen.pearl.

The Stone

Life start with nothing in hand,
But lot of love to express and gift,
And it started to flourish a bit,
From nothing to something,
The journey started to flag off.

Down from sail we start to build,
Rules of land and sea were set up,
Dividing the gaps to enlarge big enough,
We missed out to show love and care,
Now after everything we lack the hood.

The feelings to other soul of life,
The respect we give away to fight,
All have changed so much till now.
After all gains we still miss out peace,
Hearts filled with hatred to poison.

This is not what should happen around,
It's not what we all wish upon,
Time is still so lengthy to chance,
That we can write the letters out of love,
To see and accept everything around.

Mohua Chakraborty

An optimistic doer who sees the world with rose-coloured glasses and gets visible in the introvertly emited spectra.

Shadow

Walking down the 24th night lane,
Tried to touch; twas' the line.
Couldn't get how you shaped, those eighteen years being a
mystery.
Found you below the shade, under the sun, superbly dark-
bodied, ejecting mimics with fun.
An expressionless black dummy, outlining my structure,
It helped get simple freaking moves capture!
How you flared through the setting sun,
Strucking my scientific asset, making a bley.
Swear I, it couldn't slay me nor could I., for it was a forever
fiend in disguise.
Following my feed doesn't approved good at all,
Still I accepted this friend, a champ, cause it had never let me
fall.

Friendship

From rangeless fights to unraged hysterics, crushing 'that'
attitude to handling of frericks.
Following your triumphs gave memories ruthless, your
presence saturated my sorrows,
Timeless grudges, but never featuring them tomorrow.
Such a divine soul, could you be more better?
Always lifted my mood, made memories together.
Saw you do a lot of magic 'whimpatic', mode change from a
sloth to a panther,
Judiciously careless, but never made me apathetic.
Don't talk of caring, we be homies to another render.
Gifts of morals doesn't portray when the gang is around, any
clashes, any 'dangals', check it out dude! you'll be taken
down.
Tom-jerry, oggy-jack are not just characters, building
bonds with such goals are splendor.
Words can't describe, relation so pure, nothing is
inaccessible, cause there can never be such a great guard

Samikhya Swain (Ikhya)

Ikhya hails from Odisha. Currently, she is a student of class 12. She loves inking because it gives peace to her heart. She is not only a passionate writer but also a painter, YouTuber and photographer. You can connect with her using her Instagram ID @triggered.ladki or simply drop a mail at samikhya123swain@gmail.com

A Part Of Me

A part of me was lost!
I tried...
I tried...
I tried...
And tried !!!
But at last
I can't gave up so fast!

Running behind something,
That was never mine
Like he was the only thing
For which I always whine.

But I can't make someone love me back
Like the way I do.

(2)

It was a Long Time since I fell in love with you
But still I was unable to see the devil behind your handsome
face.
The alive beast who was ready to tear me apart.
Write-up 3 with Title
The other side

It's all because I don't say,
You don't try to hear the cries of my heart.
It's all because I am happy,
You boil in your own rage.
It's all because I don't scream,
You think my heart doesn't aches.
But still they all are ignored!
You know why?
Because still I give a shit to your intentions.

Punita Sinha

Punita Sinha considers herself a Learner and an observer and her first love to be music and words . She isn't good at telling out loud her feelings therefore,she writes . She's someone who can travel miles alone only if she's earphones on ,a camera of any sort to capture and something to write upon.

Imperfections

You see my flaws
And still manage to love me,
Those flaws that
I don't even like in me!

Somedays I'm angry,
Somedays I become sad,
No reasons but only
End up being that.

You stay there through
Each one of these,
Making me love myself
Even more and fighting for me!

Sometimes I just wish
To be a little like you,
Learn a little self love
And not give up only for you!

I never knew I would find
More than lover,a teacher in you
Well now I think ,
I am lucky to have met you;
Cause you my love
Don't shadow my imperfections,
You make me grow
You teach me to be me and
Still ,still love me even after knowing
That there are imperfections in me!!

Lover

To the lover who I'm going to love,

I know you'll be all-ready in
Love with someone else,
But would you give us chance
And make our story the best ?

I know things would be lovely
And so romantic at the start,
But would you continue to love me
if I sometimes try to escape?

I know you would not be used to
care about anyone after that heartbreak,
But would you still try to pamper me
And make me feel great ?

I know people watch their lovers
Dancing in the rain ,
But would you do a favour
And dance with me in the same?

I know with me in your life,
You'll have a lot of troubles,
But would ya chose to remain ,
I promise I'll be there for you forever??

Maitreyee

She is Maitreyee. She is bubbly, scintilating and ambitious. She holds expertise in story telling, micro tales and also knows how to weave words into beautiful poetries. Besides she is also a foodie and loves cooking as well.

My Dream~

We all have dreams.
Maybe yours is to be the best at something in school or at work, at a sport or some other passion. Or to make the trip somewhere in the world that you've been thinking about for years now and probably this 2020 put a damper on your plans! Or maybe to improve your financial situation, social skills, find that special someone or to get into great shape. Well every great dream begins with a dreamer.. And the dreamer is right here!! I have a dream too. No, not that disney princess dream ofcourse!
When i was young i dreamt of becoming the richest of all since i thought money could buy anything, atleast my favourite of all candies at that age! But as i grew older i realised that the job of doctors allured me the most. And then i was sure what i wish to do ahead in life! They are considered equivalent to God and are highly respected in the society.
But you know what's the funniest thing i found about dreams? Though they are lovely, but they are just dreams. Fleeting, ephemeral, pretty! And they donot come true just because you dream them. It's hard work that makes things happen. It's hard work that creates change!
And i am sure i will definitely make the grade!
Do you know so many of our dreams first seem Impossible.. then Seem Improbable and then when we summon the will... they soon seem Inevitable.. and this is exactly i will do! No i will not give up! Even if i come up against any problem... I will remind myself that FAILURE is not the opposite of Success.. it's just a Part Of It!.

Yes I Have A Dream And I Will Achieve It!

Adarsh Kumar Priyadarshi

Adarsh Kumar Priyadarshi is a school going boy form a small town called Hajipur, Bihar. His father servers the nation in Indian Army. And his mother is a housemarker. He is co-author of 40+ anthology As he is proud to be the son of a loyal army man so he too wants to do something great for his mother-land. As he has a great zeal in medical field so he is currently even struggling with his journey to reach his destination, his goal i.e. to be a renowned doctor. He always thanks his parents, teachers, friend and God for what he is now.

His debut, book will be launched soon.

You can follow him on Instagram (@adarsh_priyadarshi_03)

Friendship

Childhood is the time when we make friends.
The friends with no boundaries.

Some friends are
Like the Carbon
They are with you in fear of the storm...!

Some friends are
Like the Chlorine
You have to sacrifice your everything...!

Some friends are
Like the fluorine,
The farther you go, the more you fight...!

But some friendships too
They are what they mean.
They are the ones who makes
Your childhood full of memories.

Avi Srivastava

He is an engineering student aimed to make his name in computer world...
Poetry is not only is his hobby but also a way to express his feelings....

Time To Shine.....

A day will come when we will shine...
A sweet house and a dream car will be mine.....
All our struggles and problems will get monetize.....
A new happy life, completely sanitised will arise......

We don't have time stone to peep into future ....
Neither we can go back to save the nature.....
All we can do is utilize the time....
Because it is the time to shine.....

यारी....

हर मर्ज़ की दवा है उनका साथ होना....
हर मुसीबत का समाधान है उनका साथ होना....
कहूँ उन्हें मैं आफत या कहूँ फिर आदत...
कुछ करू या ना करू, पर करू उनकी ही इबादत......

कर रहा हूँ मैं बाते उन यारो की, जिनके बिना है जीवन अधूरा....
जिनके दिमाग भले हो आधे, पर उनपे विश्वास है पूरा.....
ना होती जो उनसे बातें, लगता है बेकार हर पल....
उनके होने से हर तकलीफ़ पल में हो जाती हैं हल.....

काफ़ी उलझ सी गई है ये ज़िन्दगी....

न जाने किस ओर बढ़ती चली जा रही,मानो आत्मनिर्भर हो गई है
जिंदगी.....
सही मौके का इंतज़ार करने को नही बल्कि मौका खुद बनाने को
कह रही है जिंदगी......
बंद पिंजरे में फड़फड़ाते पक्षी को खुले आसमान में उड़ाने को कह
रही ज़िन्दगी....

ये ज़िन्दगी बड़ी ज़ालिम है यारो, नही देगी आसानी से जीने....
जो न चले तुम इसके हिसाब से, बेकार है बहाना खून-पसीने.....

Harshit Kumar

Harshit Kumar is a founder of its own world of writing. He is not a professional Writer . He is Medical Aspirant , along with the power to melt anyone with its written compositions. It says that anyone can build a hut but it takes time to build a palace, so you must have patience.

His views towards writing..

Writing is the best way to express our emotions like love, lust, anger, temper, happiness, loneliness almost every type of feelings that we won't like to share with anyone. Nothing can make us more happier & satisfactory than writing, as it helps to bring out our deep thoughts and make others to understood ours' feelings as well . Writers have the power to create their own world of imagination, which they can write about of, which makes them The Brahma'(The Creater) of their's own world…

Along with this, he is an animal lover and a nature explorer (want to explore the world & read the mind of nature..).

Kya Mujhe Pta Hai ??

Waise to zindgi me kai utar chdhaav chlte hi rehte hai , inhi utaar
chdhaav me se hamare pas kuch aise pal, kuch aise kisse hote hai
jo hume ye bta dete hai hamare liye kya sahi hai or kya galat …
Bhut dukh hota hai jb koi apna hume chor jata hai , lekin wo hume
hamari zindgi ka sabse jaroori path pdhaa ke jata hai ,Apne aur
Paray ka path bs zaroorat hai to use sahi se smjhne ki …

Jane wala to chla hi jata hai,
Magar rula to wo apno ko hi jata hai
Dukh me to apne hi sath hote hai
Jo dukh me hi sath na hua , wo apna hi kha se..

Jane wale ko to mano jaise wo ek gehri nind me so gye
Ban na tha jinhe hakikat ,wo sapne kuch samay ke liye akele ho
gye
Pr dukh to is baat ka hai ,
Jinhe kehte the wo apna jigri ,
Wo jigri bhi bs do pal naam ke liye ro gye …

Tum apne dukh se dukhi nahi ho ,
Bs dusre ki khushi bardhaash nahi tumhe
Jiski antim yatra me tum gye gye the
Us se aakhri mulakat tk yaad nahi tumhe

Majboot bhi tum bn jaoge
Is sadme se bhi nikl jaoge
Agar raste me fir bhi yahi kaante rahe ,
To syd ek baar fir yahi itihaas dohraoge……

Neha Singhania

Hello,introducing Neha Singhania. She is Pursuing CS and a good dancer and a dance tutor too.Writing is her passion, and she want to be a good known writter. she is a part of many anthologies as a co-author .she always try to write on undefined feelings.. she is having her own instagram page @ dil-e-ehsasss

रिश्तों का आधार -विश्वास

समय लग जाता है भरोशा कमाने में
और टूटने में केवल छड़ भर
रिश्तों में हमेशा सच बोलो
क्योंकि सच से ही बनता है विश्वास
एक झूठ के लिए सौ झुठ
फिर झूठ से टूटेगा विश्वास

ये तो ऐसी दौलत है
जो मिले न सभी को
जो मिले जाए तुम्हे
रखना सम्हाले इसे

जो समझे तुम्हरी चूपी का राज़
और गुस्से के पीछे का प्यार
इन्हें पे करना विश्वास
जो जाने तुम्हरी झूठी मुस्कुराहट का राज़

विश्वास ही जरूरी है हर रिश्ते में
जैसे खाने में नमक
बिना इसके नही कोई अर्थ रिश्तों का
जैसे बेस्वाद का है खाना बिन नमक

बनाये रखना किसी का विश्वास
और सोच के करना किसी वे विश्वास
झूठी दुनिया मे लोग बार बार कहते है
TRUST में Once More यार।

Siya Golani

Siya golani is a creative writer. She has inclination to positive aspects of life. She is a confident presenter who keeps her views very subtle but firmly. She evokes her messages and effectively engages the audience through her writeups.

Precious Gift

Nature is such a wonderful creature and also a perfect
teacher.
It is precious like stone because god has made this on his
own.

It is expensive as diamond and miraculous as magical wand.
But, you get it for free and that's why you are carefree.

You are here because of nature but you are not having any
plans for future.
Your kids will ask what is grass, what are stars and where are
flowers.
What are trees and how does it look when its all green.

At that time you will feel speechless because now you are
shameless and our nature is in a big stress.

Present!

Yesterday was a history, tomorrow is a mystery, but today is a gift and that's why it's called present.

Today is the day. Get up and just do it. The magical wand of happiness is with you. Do you know what's next, what is going to happen tomorrow? I will give you the answer and the answer is NO !!No one knows about it you neither have yesterday in your hands nor have tomorrow what you have in your hand is just present you can do anything you want , but the first step is you have to start today, don't worry for tomorrow because you have already reached the half way you just have to go a few km gear up and fly.

Richie Racheeta

Richie Racheeta a twelfth grader, pursuing science who is passionate about art in any form.
Generally daydreaming, you can find her with a pen and paper giving her random thoughts various shapes and characters. Being a multipotentialite, she is enthusiastic enough to try out any possible new thing at hand. She dreams to travel to unknown places and glean the unsaid tales.

"We"

As the wind whispered our tale
In each other's ears,
We smiled n blushed
Filling the void with joy and ecstasy.

Our laughs echoed, cherishing love
As your red face flashed upon in the clouds,
I shied away, the palm covering my face.
And both of us got our best company,
As u laid ur shoulders for me to lean on.

At once the reality was turned into a dream
Defying the the distance that so had lived.
Thus, our hearts danced together,
Dreaming for the same star,
Wishing upon the same sky.

Purity dropped as oozing love,
Making each of us most truly ours.

Khushbu Rathore

An independent soul who likes to read, write, pants and design. A girl who, through poetry, expresses her feelings and enjoys comfort.

B. Ed is very talented girl with getting education. A proud girl from Pali district of Rajasthan receives her education during the day and most of her time in the night gives her time to the writing work. She is Khusbu Rathore and is delighted to be a part of this anthology

Instagram =@khushburathore1913

पहला प्यार

जब मिलती हैं निगाहे उससे तो सब कुछ धुंधला-सा लगता हैं
आती नहीं नींद और फिर ख्यालो से फिर वो जगता है
जैसे लगता हैं सब कुछ सुहाना हैं
उसके सिवा नहीं किसी का दिल में आना हैं
देखने के लिए उसको किसी बहाने से उसके घर जाना हैं
और हो जाता उसका वो दीवाना हैं
उससे सारी बाते करना, उसकी फिक्र जताना।
उसको प्यार भरे नामो से पुकारना।
अपनी हमेशा पलकों पे बिठाना।
अगर कुछ दफ़े के लिए बात ना करें तो नाराज़गी जताना
उसकी मासूमियत पे सब कुछ हार जाना।
नाराज़गी भुलाकर उसको सीने से लगाना।
उसकी पसंद की सारी चीज़े करना !
उसको खोने से डरना !
होता हैं कुछ अलग ही भूत सवार !
ऐसा होता हैं पहला प्यार !

Sachcha Pyaar

Zindgi m sachcha Pyar hota ek bar h....
Pyar ek khushnuma ehsas h....
Pyar to udas chehro ko bhi khush krde ....
Itni takat pyar k paas h.

Kya likhu m pyar k bare m.....
Is ehsas pr likhne k lye alfaaz kam mere paas h...
Zindgi m agar Pyar ho jay ek baar..
Iske baad na baki rehne wali koi aas h...

Chahat h pyar krne ki ek baar...
Kya pata kitni saase bachi ab hamare paas h...
Kehte h pyar kya nahi jata bs ho jata h...
Na jane kitne dil kiske paas h..

Pyar ko to yuhi badnaam krte h log...
Badnaam ise kar hawas ka naam dete h log...
Par wo kya Jaane....
Isse badkr na koi khushnuma ehsaas h.

Anmol Chugh Dildard

Anmol Chugh Dildard is a student of b.tech civil engineering at St. Soldier group of institutions. He is from Jalandhar City, Punjab. His hobby is to read and write thoughts and poetries. His aim is to become a good civil engineering and poetry writer.

करिश्में का इंतज़ार

उस करिश्में का इंतज़ार है,
जब वो आकर मुझसे कहेंगे,
कि मुझे तुम्हारी जरूरत है,
मुझे उस करिश्में का इंतज़ार है,
जब वो आकर मुझसे कहेंगे,
कि मुझे भी तुमसे प्यार है..!!

होंसला

ये तेरा होंसला है,
कि तू ऐसी ज़िन्दगी जी रहा है,
अपनों के ही हाथों से ज़हर पी रहा है,
ये तेरा होंसला है,
कि तू अपने जीवन की हर मुश्किल से लड़ रहा है,
दुखों के होते हुए भी और दुखों कि मांग कर रहा है,
धोखेबाजों के हाथों पल पल मर रहा है..!!

Sreelakshmi Viswam

Sreelakshmi is a 19 year old studying im army college of dental sciences.An aspiring author and voracious reader she lives in the tales she reads

Summer

Let my fury like a flame throwing dragon turn air to wisps
Let forest fires wrinkle earth and her leafy hair to cinders
Let thunderstorms pierce the clouds
Let the roaring sea deafen the vacillating voices
Let the ground quiver violently from the release of seismic energy
The fault lines in our tectonic growth

Monsoon

I knew the storm was coming
The lightning was unseen
But it fortold the thunder

The wind howls like a forlorn lover
Terrified trees tremble
Haunted by the dancing shadows
On unpaved roads of the past
Where drops of heaven fall on green harps

How i wish to unleash my fury
like the unhedged sky
To cast gloom on mortals and ravage that which hinders my path
Release my pain slowly and surely like the incessant rain than an impulsive cloudburst

Empty

Steal the scent of a rose
Silence the song of a bird
Rob the pearls from a clam
Plunder honey from a bee
Veil the moon from a starless sky
Strip the wings of a butterfly
Blow out the fire in my soul.
Like a lock without a key
They all feel empty

Saloni Santosh Gawas

She is from Goa.
She is a Science student who completed her 12th std this year. She has taken a step forward for her 1st year of undergraduate course.
She is passionate about writing since she was in 6th std.
She is a night sky viewer and loves to write about stars.
As writing is passion which is quite rare and sometimes left unnoticed, she got great support from her friends and now she is introduced to write in anthologies.

Mesmerizing Childhood

Sunrise with Mom's voice
Little feet towards school was joy
Those unique games and weird photographs
Along with Grandma's tales in moonlight sky..

Alarm clock stole that morning's soul
School is same but heavy minds took away that glow
Kids became busy on mobiles
N those Grandma's tales are lost in dark nights.

Modern technology made kids moody
Having less moral values
We are lucky to spend our childhood
In the era of Golden Eves...

Little Angel

A special part to remember
Which became a beautiful memory
Almost like a dream it was
That little soul's lovely entry

Waiting on the doorstep
On a single call u came running
Sitting beside for late nights
Your cute yawns while I was studying

Sometimes when things went low
Even before the tear fell
You came and played with my clothes
Really those feelings how could you know

My hand was your pillow
And your heart was full of love
Many times you slept in my lap
Now I hope..
In God's arms you are safe

Sanoj Kumar

He is an engineer, started writing two years back never imagined that people would like it, and feel his emotions as theirs. He also likes to express other's feelings and always try to change other's mindsets in a better way through his writings. Nowadays he is a member of many writing communities and earned lots of certificates through his writings. His first book as an author is launched from a " poetry world organization " named as " सफ़र, जिन्दगी का ". " Fam-Bond in lockdown " is his first anthology as a compiler and editor while he is a co-author of many anthologies.
You can see his poetry on Instagram @the_hidden_writer_sk
And an article on blogger @http://safarzindagikask.blogspot.com
Contact him through his mail id @thehiddenwritersk@gmail.com

वो शहर

छूट गया वो शहर, जहां हम खुल कर जिया करते थे।
गैरों को ही अपना मान, अपनों को स्मरण किया करते थे।

वो मोहल्ला, वो गली, अब बस उनकी यादें ही रह गई।
घर से दूर जो भी रिश्ते बनाए थे, शायद वो भी अब वहीं छूट गई।

वो राशन वालो का उधार हो, या गर्ल्स हॉस्टल वाला प्यार।
समय के साथ धुंधला हो जायेगा, हमारा कॉलेज वाला परिवार।

चाय के बहाने अड्डा जमाते थे, जो पीते नहीं, वो भी साथ आते थे।
मॉल के बाहर बैठकी लगाकर, एक दूसरे का मजाक बनाते थे।

हमउम्र रहने के कारण, सबका सुख दुख समझते थे।
प्यार हुआ हो या दिल टूटा हो, हम बेहीजक साझा करते थे।

डिग्री मिलते ही सब खत्म हो गया, पता नहीं वो पल कहां खो गया।
हम तो भविष्य संवारने आ गए, पर हमारा नादान मन वहीं रह गया।

Sahina Ghugha

Sahina Ghugha is 20 year old b.com student at Saurashtra university, Rajkot. She is from Jamnagar city of Gujarat. She is state level champion in poetry competition 2017. She want to do something for society through her pen.

दिल कुछ कहेना चाहता है

आज तुमसे ये दिल कुछ कहेना चाहता है,
आखरी धड़कन तक तुम्हारे साथ रहेना चाहता है।

फिज़ाए जो तुमसे छूकर गुजरती है,
ये मिट्टी सा उसमे उड़ना चाहता है।
बन सके जो तुम्हारे दामन का टुकड़ा,
तो ये बदन से तुम्हारे जुड़ना चाहता है।
नींद में देखे गए एक ख़्वाब सा,
तुम्हारी रातो में साथ रहेना चाहता है।
आज तुमसे ये दिल कुछ कहेना चाहता है।

वीरान रेगिस्तान में भटक रहा है,
तुम्हे पानी की आस बनाना चाहता है।
तुम्हे समेट कर खुद में ये दिल,
तुमको आखरी सांस बनाना चाहता है।
जो ले चलो तुम अपने साथ इसे,
तो तुममें लहरों सा बहेना चाहता है।
आज तुमसे ये दिल कुछ कहेना चाहता है।

Ujjwal Shree

Ujjwal Shree with her pen name Neha Gupta is from Patna, Bihar She is an avid writer, poetess, and artist. She loves to play with words and write from the depth of her heart. She always express her emotions through words rather than saying. She generally writes about Motivation, emotions, pain and abstract. Writing helps her to survive in her worst phase of life. Writing is just like breathing to her because when she feels depressed she used to write her feelings.

Follow her on Instagram : @Shree22349

Email Id : ng223494@gmail.com

Paths of Fear

I was safe. Alone, in the comforts of ignorance, i had nothing to fear. I had taken all expected precautions and avoided the dark alleyways and men of suspect character. I had in my ignorance, given a face and a name to fear. I had given him a type, a religion and even a nationality. I had classified and believed to have analysed everything about him, I wanted to defeat him and never again give-in to his whims.

But he took me by surprise. He did not hide, he came as a friend. He avoided the dark alleyways, just like me. He spoke with words which sounded like wisdom, voice which seemed too appealing. He made it impossible to fight him because he was born of the hate within me. I could never defeat him now. I had myself, become all of that, which I most feared.

Hidden Scars

Heart full of stars
With the hidden scars
 Each one witnessing an indelible story
Each one crowning her with glory
In the abyss of every scar
Lies silhouette of the past afar....

Crack of dawn

And with that crack of dawn,
an unusual sound hit her eardrums.
The same old boresome chirp of the cuckoo
found a new voice to sing with in nest.

"At least one of us is enduring brightness,"
taking a sigh of relief she closed the curtains again...

Hema Kirthiga J

She is Hema Kirthiga J, and her pen name is sparkle. She is professionally a psychologist and passionately a writer. She heals others but writing heals her. She is writer, reader, orator and a believer. She is from Chennai. She lives by the principal of inspire and be inspired. She writes her heart and soul and she deeply believes that the depth of her heart and the nib of her pen are soulfully connected. Writing is an art and she is a proud artist. She loves what she does and loves what she writes. You can reach her at

Instagram- @the_pen_queen
Email- inker.sparkle@gmail.com
Yourquote – JKM

To the Love Of My Life!

You will remain my dearest!
Ever and forever!
You will be the sweetheart of my life!
Now and always!
The sunshine of my strom!
The water of my drought!
The painkiller of my life!
The lucky charm of my day!!
The sweetest smiles belong to you!
The smartest brain belongs to you!
The fittest body belongs to you!
The super heart belongs to you!
Oh my dear!
I love you

Sanjida Khan

Sanjida is a student at Vidhaan Public School. She likes to write and sketch..

Dosti Se Pyaara Koi Rishta Nhi..

Dosti ka koi mol nhii..
Vishvaas bhi hota hai..
Pyaar bhi hota hai...
Pr koi mol nhi hota hai...
Anmol hoti hai dosti..
Rishta ye khoon ka nhii..
Rishta ye dilo ka hota hai..
Rishta sharton ka nhi..
Rishta atoot vishvas ka hota hai...
Zindagi mein ek dost se pyaara dujaa khaan koi hota hai..

Bachpan Ki Dosti..

Dost to boht hain pr bachpan ke dost kuch khaas hote hain..
Jese kabhi bachpan nhi bhula jata..
Wese hi us bachpan ka vo dost nhi bhula jaata..
Vo baarsih me saath khelna..
Dhup mein rait ke teelon pr nikalna..
Kaagaz ki kashtii ko paani mein bhana...
Vo saath mein chocalate khana..
Kabhi nhi bhul paate hum..
Bachpan ke dosto se rishta kuch aisa hota hai....
Kabhi na bhula paane waale us bachpan jesa hota hai...
Bachpan ke dosto ka vo rishta anmol hota hai..

Shivansh Sharma

He is shivansh sharma . Basically from indore but persuing MBA(Marketing &Hr) in mysore karnataka . He always have passion towards writng the thoughts which comes in to his mind . A hardcore fodiee as he belongs to indore . He is the one who is always ready to help to his near ones .His life revolves around his family and friends. He is always self motivated , enthusiastic and person with positive vibes .He is co-author of 10+ books and compiler of 1 book . His only belief is just live happily and enjoy every moment of life . You can contact him on ig@shivanshrockzzzzz

गलतियां

बेशक कुछ गलती मेरी होगी,
पर कुछ गलतियां तेरी भी होगी ,
बेशक हमारी तरह तुम भी रोए होंगे,
        यकीन है हमे यह ,
तुम भी तड़प होंगी उन रात के अंधेरे में
हमारी तरह बीते लम्हों को याद करके ,
उन लम्हों के साथ ,
हम भी याद आए होंगे ,

बेशक कुछ गलती मेरी होगी,
पर कुछ गलतियां तेरी भी होगी
वो रातों की वो प्यार भरी बातें,
वो रातों की शरारतें ,
जिसमे ना जाने नींद कहां खो जाती थी,
बेशक हमारी तरह तुम्हे भी याद होगी ,
की हमारी मोहब्बत की सीमा नहीं थी ,
किस कदर मेरी आंखे भीग जाया करती है
बुरा ना में था ना तुम थी ,
बेशक कुछ गलती मेरी होगी,
पर कुछ गलतियां तेरी भी होगी

रात के उन पलो में बहुत भीगी होगी ,
जब सबसे ज्यादा हमरी जरूरत थी,
रात के आगोश में तुम भी नहीं
सो पाते होंगे हमारी तरह

बेशक कुछ गलती मेरी होगी,
पर कुछ गलतियां तेरी भी होगी

इन गलतियों के कारण ही आज
हम जुदा हुए है और तड़पे जा रहे है।।

इन गलतियों के कारण ही आज
हम जुदा हुए है और तड़पे जा रहे है।।

Anurag Anand

Anurag Anand is a teenage author whose debut book called, 'ELEVATION OF LIFE' got published in 2018, when he was in 10th standard. He was born on 22nd June 2003 in Bihar. Currently, he is a student of 12th standard in 'TIMES WORLD SCHOOL, Dehradun'. He is very grateful to the Almighty for everything he has. He thank his parents and grandparents for their affection and support in providing a better education. He thank his buddies too for constantly supporting him. In an interview when asked, how did he come up with a book at an early age; he responded, "it's not the age factor which barricades one's journey to follow his/her passion; be it teenage or old age. The barricade is probably in our heads, which should be broken & one should come up for his/her goal despite of blaming anything." I wish him all the luck and success in his life. I hope his work of writing entertains and enlightens all its readers.To connect, you can follow him on Twitter(@anurag_anand5) as well as on Instagram(@anurag_anand_official)
"God has been kind enough." :)

Even Such People Exist

Why are they so manipulative?
And not as good to be cooperative
I don't understand-
'Why don't they understand.'
I want to see their hands
With all of them together
Rather cutting each others' feather

They manipulate
Of course because to each other they hate
And they do this in such a way
I don't know how to say.
An addition to a topic can get on top
They can even call a cop

They incident seems to be nothing
At last when came to know
After investigating
And interrogating
So, why such melodrama did they sing?
Today I came to know
Even Such People Exist
On the top of the list to manipulate
And hate.

Do they enjoy doing so?
Perhaps they would be so free to do so.

Flairs and Glairs, a platform by a student for the students. We are esteemed youth struggling to carve out our path for our future and we follow a basic mindset Since everyone is not born with all-round skills. Joining hands with people who are born to execute it with perfection is the best way to evolve. Self-Evolution is the need of the hour but, evolving as a community is what we strive for. The initiative as kickstarted by, Founder-Mr. Shubham Shah with the motive to utilize the skillset and talent of writing has now a team of 10+ people who are actively participating into newer forms of learning and discovering talents among youngsters. We Provide platform and services like Publishing opportunities, Open mics, Workshops, Hands-on training. Operating with Brand Name Of Flairs and Glairs (Publication House), we offer the chance of elevating a passionate writer to an esteemed author With Brand name Teekhe Zasbaaat, We bring to you an opportunity to get accustomed with the Public Speaking and Presenting of Thoughts along with regular challenges to brush up your inking spirit. The newest initiative to extend our services we introduced in a new writing Platform- The Glittering Fables and Ink Over Tears.

We Choose to Fly Like A Falcon than to be a

Leg Pulling Crab.

To Know More: Infoline – 7781900870
Mail Us At-
flairsandglairs@gmail.com / info@flairsandglairs.in
Or Visit is at
www.flairsandglairs.com / www.flairsandglairs.in
Social Handles- @flairsandglairs @teekhezasbaaat